Wild Things

Written by Cynthia Maxwell
Illustrated by Stephen Axelsen

An easy-to-read SOLO
for beginning readers

LEXILE™ 420

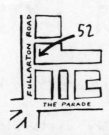

Omnibus Books
A.C.N. 000 614 577
52 Fullarton Road, Norwood, South Australia 5067
part of the SCHOLASTIC GROUP
Sydney · Auckland · New York · Toronto · London
www.scholastic.com.au

First published 2000
Reprinted 2000

Cover design by Lyn Mitchell
Typeset by Clinton Ellicott, Adelaide
Printed and bound by Hyde Park Press, Adelaide

National Library of Australia Cataloguing-in-Publication entry
Maxwell, Cynthia, 1959– .
Wild things.
ISBN 1 86291 426 5.
I. Axelsen, Stephen. II. Title. (Series: Solos
(Norwood, S. Aust.)).

A823.3

For Danni – C.M.

For Trippy, our wild thing – S.A.

Chapter 1

"My friend Sam brought his wild animals to school today," Carla told Dad at tea time.

Dad gulped. "Wild animals! How scary!" he said.

"*I* wasn't scared," said Carla. "Sam had to go away, and he couldn't take his animals with him. It was really very sad."

"So what did Sam do with his wild animals?" asked Dad.

"He had to give them away," said Carla.

"Oh, poor Sam," said Dad. "Where are they now?"

"In our bathroom," said Carla.

"Our bathroom! Wild things in our bathroom!" said Dad.

"Yes," said Carla. "And they're starving hungry. Come and help me feed them."

Chapter 2

"Where did Sam get all these animals?" asked Dad, peering around the bathroom door.

"He found them in the creek," said Carla.

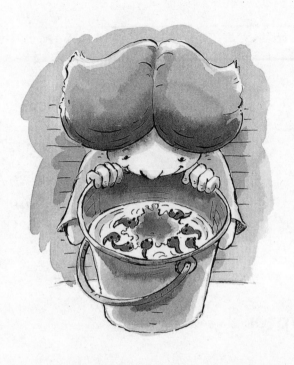

The smallest of the creatures
were in a bucket of water. Carla
put some lettuce in the bucket.
She watched the swarm of black
tadpoles gobble the green leaves.

The biggest creature was in a fish tank. Carla rolled mince meat into a ball and dropped it into the water. In the fish tank was a yabby, waving its big blue claws.

"Careful it doesn't nip you," said Dad.

The last of the wild creatures was
a frog. Carla didn't need to feed
the frog. It caught its own dinner.

"I'm a bit scared of frogs," Dad whispered.

He tiptoed away from the bathroom door. "Good froggy, nice
froggy," he said.

Chapter 3

Next day the fish tank was empty.

"The yabby has gone. It must have climbed out of the tank," Carla told Dad.

"Oh-oh," said Dad.

"Maybe it's going to rain," said Carla. "Sam says that yabbies try to climb out of the tank when it rains."

They looked out the window. The sky was blue.

"It's not going to rain," said Dad.

Dad and Carla had to find the yabby.

They looked under the hand basin.

They looked
in the toilet.

They looked under the beds and behind the doors.

They searched the whole house.

Carla found the yabby behind the fridge. It looked scared, and its big blue claws were covered in cobwebs and dust.

"Just look at that yabby," said Dad. "It's so scared its eyes are popping out of its head."

"Yabbies' eyes are always popping out of their heads," Carla told him.

Dad reached in behind the fridge
and tried to pick the yabby up.

It nipped him.
"Ow, ow, ow!" cried Dad.

Carla gently picked up the yabby
with the kitchen tongs and plopped
it back in the fish tank.

She stuck a band-aid on Dad's finger.

"Don't be upset, Dad," she said. But Dad *was* upset.

Chapter 4

"The tadpoles are hungry again,"
Carla told Dad that afternoon.
"We have to buy them some more
lettuce."

"I didn't know tadpoles ate so much," Dad grumbled.

They put on their hats to walk to the shop. Carla put on a rain-coat too.

"Why are you wearing a rain-coat?" asked Dad. "It's not raining."

"The yabby thinks it's going to rain," said Carla.

"Nonsense," said Dad.

As they were walking back from the shop, a grey cloud covered the blue sky. Rain started to fall.

Dad and Carla ran home as fast as they could.

Dad was soaked to the skin.

"Don't be mad," said Carla. But Dad *was* mad.

Chapter 5

"Help! Help!" cried Dad.

He was in the bathroom, brushing his teeth. The frog was sitting on his hand.

"Don't be scared," Carla said.
But Dad *was* scared.

The frog hopped up Dad's arm.
"Get it off me," begged Dad.

"Keep still," ordered Carla. Very slowly, she reached for the frog. It jumped onto Dad's shoulder.

Carla tried to grab it, but the frog
was too quick. *Splat!* It landed on
Dad's head.

"Aargh!" yelled Dad. He ran down
the hall, flapping his hands wildly.

"Stop, Dad!" Carla chased Dad around the house. "The frog's still on your head!" she shouted.

Dad stopped. Carla caught the frog.

"Aargh!" yelled Dad, and he kept on running.

Chapter 6

Dad said that living with wild creatures was too scary. He told Carla she couldn't keep them.

"Don't be sad, Carla," he said.
But Carla *was* sad.

"We'll give these wild things to someone else," said Dad, "and you can have a normal pet. A nice pet, something cute and furry."

Chapter 7

On Saturday Dad carried out a
table and an umbrella and put them
on the footpath.

Carla wrote a big sign.

FREE To GOOD HOMES
Tadpoles
one frog one yabby

Two girls on roller-blades skated over.

"Tadpoles, yuck!" they yelled as they sped off.

All day Carla tried to give the creatures away. Lots of people stopped for a look, but nobody wanted to take the wild things home with them.

Late in the afternoon a girl stopped at Carla's table.

"Hi, I'm Tashi," she said.

FREE TO GOOD HOMES
Tadpoles
one frog one yabby

Dad called out from the house, "Have you found good homes for those wild creatures yet, Carla?"

"*I* know a good home for them," said Tashi.

Chapter 8

They walked to Tashi's house. Tashi carried the yabby in a bucket. Dad carried the tadpoles in a big jar. Carla carried the frog in her lunch box.

At the bottom of Tashi's
back yard was a creek.

"What a good idea! We'll put the
creatures back in the creek. That's
where they belong," said Carla.

"They'll be happy there," said
Tashi.

The frog hopped onto a lily pad.

The tadpoles swam into a shallow pool.

The yabby burrowed into the sand until all you could see of it were its eyes.

Chapter 9

"Dad says I can have another pet now," Carla said to Tashi as they walked back from the creek.

"You could have one of my pets,"
said Tashi.

"Is it cute and furry?" asked Dad.

"Oh yes," said Tashi.

Tashi went into her house and came out with a box. She gave it to Carla, who took off the lid.

"Oh, it's so cute!" Carla cried. She showed it to Dad.

"Look, Dad! It's the cutest, furriest pet I've ever seen!"

Cynthia Maxwell

When I was eight I had a pet huntsman spider called Herman. Most people were scared of him, but I thought he was cute.

I don't have Herman any more, and my wildest pets are frogs and tadpoles. Every summer frogs lay masses of eggs in our swimming pool. I scoop up the eggs, put them in a small pond and feed the tadpoles when they hatch. I've got hundreds of tadpoles. They eat a lot of lettuce!

The idea for *Wild Things* came from the frogs and their tadpoles, my nephew's pet yabby, Houdini – and Herman the huntsman.

Stephen Axelsen

I am not a very brave person. Many, many things worry me a great deal. But when it comes to small creatures I am a lot braver than Carla's dad.

When I was younger and sillier (not so very long ago), I used to collect harmless medium-sized spiders and throw them at my wife or daughter. Their squealing and shrieking was very funny, but I got into a lot of trouble and had to stop.

Now I am a sensible, grown-up illustrator. But I would still like to throw a very small spider at an author, and see what happens!